The Arts

JACK LONDON

rourke biographies

The Arts

JACK LONDON

by
JOHN POWELL

Rourke Publications, Inc.
Vero Beach, Florida 32964

To Grady, Tessa, and Ellen
and
All the great kids in the Fort LeBoeuf schools.

∞ The paper used in this book conforms to the American National Standard for Permanence of Paper for Printed Library Materials, Z39.48-1984.

Library of Congress Cataloging-in-Publication Data
Powell, John Douglas, 1954-
   Jack London / written by John Powell.
      p.   cm. — (Rourke biographies. The arts)
   Includes bibliographical references and index.
   Summary: A biography of the American author and adventurer who wrote about the ruthless forces of nature.
   ISBN 0-86625-486-2 (alk. paper)
   1. London, Jack, 1876-1916—Juvenile literature.   2. Authors, American—20th century—Biography—Juvenile literature.   [1. London, Jack, 1876-1916.   2. Authors, American.]   I. Jack London.   II. Title.   III. Series.
PS3523.046Z855   1993
813'.52—dc20
[B]   92-46766
                                                               CIP
                                                               AC

PRINTED IN THE UNITED STATES OF AMERICA

Contents

Color Illustrations

The Arts

JACK LONDON

Chapter 1

Looking for the Last Frontier

In less than twenty years, Jack London produced two hundred short stories, fifty books, and more than four hundred pieces of nonfiction. His writing has been described as "absolutely original," and his works have been more widely translated than those of any other author from the United States. Yet as one critic has argued, "the greatest story Jack London ever wrote was the story he lived."

London's stories of adventure in faraway places caught the imagination of the reading public at a time when books and magazines were filled with sentimental stories of home life. His tales of the rugged life aboard whaling ships in the Bering Sea or in the gold camps of the Klondike region of Canada attracted the attention of a public craving heartier fare in its reading. London loved and respected animals, and some of his best-loved works, such as *The Call of the Wild*, are written from an animal's point of view. London excelled in the "plain style" of naturalism, which captured the raw energy of people grappling with the larger forces of nature.

The Story Jack London Lived

Yet writing was only a part of London's life. He grew up in the poorer districts of Oakland and San Francisco during the late nineteenth century, when there was little job security. "Survival of the fittest" was the watchword. Theodore Roosevelt, who became president in 1901, represented an American ideal in preaching that a person's goal should be "the life of strenuous endeavor," rather than a life of ease. Few people lived such strenuous lives, out of both necessity and

Jack London always seemed happiest and most at ease when on board a sailing ship. (Trust of Irving Shepard)

choice, as Jack London. At the age of thirteen he became, in his own words, a "work-beast" in a cannery; at fifteen, a pirate stealing oysters in San Francisco Bay; at seventeen, an able-bodied seaman in the Arctic; at eighteen, a hobo trekking cross-country; and at twenty-one, a prospective miner, penetrating the hostile Klondike region of Canada in search of gold. What set London apart was his ability to bring such experiences to life for a mass of people who seldom stirred from their little worlds of home and workplace.

The first article London sold was "Story of a Typhoon off the Coast of Japan" (1893), an account of a harrowing experience aboard the seal-hunting ship *Sophia Sutherland*. His year in the Klondike furnished him with materials for the works that would make him an internationally famous author, including *The Son of the Wolf* (1900), *The God of His Fathers & Other Stories* (1901), *Children of the Frost* (1902), *The Call of the Wild* (1903), and *White Fang* (1907). Before reaching the age of thirty, Jack London was the best-selling and highest-paid writer in the United States.

London and Social Reform

London was also a pioneer in the literature of social protest. This part of his writing, too, was based upon his own life experiences. The industrialization of America had produced great wealth during the last quarter of the nineteenth century. However, it was concentrated in the hands of a few "captains of industry" and was bought at the price of low wages and dangerous conditions for factory workers. In 1894, London tramped across the United States with Jacob Coxey's army of the unemployed, who were marching to Washington, D.C., to demand that the government treat workers more fairly. These experiences were later memorialized in *The Road* (1907).

Shortly after this journey, he began regularly to study how economics affects the way people live together in society.

13

London read through dozens of important books on the subject. He became excited about socialism, which was popular among intellectuals in the early twentieth century. Socialists believe that property should be owned by large groups of people so that factory owners and landowners cannot take advantage of the workers. London was associated with various socialist groups and took an increasing interest in the ways that society was divided between the rich and poor.

In 1902 he spent six weeks in London's notorious East End, passing as a down-and-out American sailor. He gave his account of this industrial underworld in *The People of the Abyss* (1903), which was serialized in *Wilshire's*, a socialist magazine. In 1905 he wrote *War of the Classes*, which strengthened his reputation as a socialist propagandist. Until late in his life, he continued to write stories and articles for socialist publications, often without pay.

Jack (right) discusses one of his stories with a friend, George Wharton James. (Trust of Irving Shepard)

Even as a socialist, however, London could never quite give up his individuality. Although he wrote for the cause, called his socialist friends "comrade," and signed himself "yours for the revolution," frequently he was critical of socialistic methods. He continued to live according to his own code, which was opposite to the socialistic principles he preached.

A Thousand Words a Day

London's discipline could serve as an example to any young writer. He set a goal of one thousand words of finished prose each day, which allowed him to write a short novel like *The Call of the Wild* in only a month. During the last fifteen years of his life he seldom failed to achieve the daily mark. As a result, rarely a month went by that a London story was absent from the major magazines such as *Cosmopolitan* or *The Saturday Evening Post*. Collections of stories and novels were produced at the rate of almost three per year.

It is not surprising, then, that much of his work seems "half finished," as many critics have noted. London's gift and livelihood were writing, so he wrote. He wrote when he was sick, when sailing his schooner across the Pacific, and even when his imagination failed and he had to pay others for ideas.

The Jack London Credo

I would rather be ashes than dust!

I would rather that my spark should burn out in a brilliant blaze
than it should be stifled by dryrot.
I would rather be a superb meteor,
every atom of me in magnificent glow,
than a sleepy and permanent planet.
The proper function of man is to live, not to exist.
I shall not waste my days in trying to prolong them.
I shall use my time.

All the things he enjoyed most—sailing, ranching, and entertaining his friends—depended upon a steady income.

Although he claimed to write only for the money, it is clear that in a thousand-words-a-day, London was sorting through the ambiguities in his own life and nature. Writing was a kind of therapy, as it has been for great writers throughout the ages.

Jack London is perhaps best remembered as the hero of a real rags-to-riches story. He proved that the American myth of success could be realized, though not without struggle and sacrifice. Because he raised himself from poverty by his own pluck and genius, readers have forgiven many of the personal failings which plagued him throughout life. He always had a problem with drinking, and he never established close relationships with his daughters. He may have been uncertain of his own principles, but the reflection of that uncertainty in his writing has endeared him to readers around the world who are still searching for a guide through the many questions of life.

Chapter 2

An Oakland Rough

In the 1870's, Flora Wellman held séances in dimly lit San Francisco rooms. She would gather people together and attempt to contact the spirits of the dead in mysterious ceremonies. Sometimes Flora, the woman who was to be Jack London's mother, also lectured on spiritualism—the belief that the dead could communicate with the living through a person called a medium. Her small body would crouch forward, a great wig of black curls hanging to meet her awkward clothes at the shoulder. She did all this almost to the day, January 12, 1876, that John Griffith Chaney—Jack London's name at birth—was born.

Unwanted Son

Flora's common-law husband, Henry Chaney, called himself a "professor of astrology." When he discovered that she was pregnant, he left in a rage. People who knew Flora felt sorry for her and took up collections to help. Within eight months, however, she married a Civil War veteran and widower, John London, who gave his name to the young boy who would one day become the most famous writer in America.

In many ways, Flora London was a mysterious figure. Growing up wealthy in Masillon, Ohio, she had been given every advantage. Living in one of the finest houses in the city, she was trained in music and educated at a finishing school. As a result, Flora was talented, well-mannered, and a good conversationalist. She might have been matched to a conventional husband for a genteel life of ease, as most wealthy young women of her generation were. She was always impetuous, however. An attack of typhoid fever when she was twenty seems to have damaged her mind and widened the gulf separating her from her parents.

Five years later, around 1871, she packed her bags and left for the West Coast to make a living teaching music. She never communicated with her parents again. Although the reason for Flora's departure is unknown, her inability or unwillingness to reconcile with her parents may help explain why she ignored Jack and often treated him coldly. Just as she had resented her parents for forcing her into the mold of respectable young girl, now she resented Jack for forcing her into the role of mother. He stood in the way of her desire for an unregulated life. When Jack was born, she had even tried to kill herself with a pistol. Some say that her effort was half-hearted, but it was nevertheless clear that a baby was not in her plans.

Who was Jack London's father? No one knows for sure. Most likely it was Chaney, the earnest astrologer who always denied responsibility and never met Jack. It could have been one of Flora's other sexual partners, though, for she was a notorious freethinker who lived as she pleased. John London certainly was not Jack's father, but he was kind to his adopted son. He also provided a measure of stability in the shaky world of spiritualism that enveloped the mind of his emotionally erratic mother. He brought Jack along to the market or the garden, taught him how to hunt and fish, and instilled in him a lifelong love of scientific farming.

John was a caring father, but he was often too busy to spend much time with his son. Most of Jack's emotional comfort came from Virginia Prentiss, "Mammy Jennie," who was his black wet nurse, and Eliza London, his older stepsister. Eliza "adopted" him shortly after his birth, when she was eight years old. As is so often the case when a child is neglected by parents, Jack tried to compensate for the emotional void by proving his self-reliance. For the time being, however, he was too young to make his own way. He needed his family's help and security, such as it was.

On the Move

Had the Londons been more settled, Jack might have found security in being part of a community, with friends and neighbors who understood one another. Unfortunately, the family always seemed to be on the move. By the time he was a toddler, Jack had moved from a boardinghouse to a working-class apartment to an area of small farms, then back to the crowded working-class section of San Francisco. Flora, who had no taste for housework or domestic nurturing, took in a boarder whose rent paid for a Chinese servant.

When Jack and Eliza almost died from an attack of diphtheria, Eliza woke from her coma long enough to hear her mother ask, "Can the two of them be buried in the same coffin, doctor, to save expenses?" Fortunately, John London was frantically searching for a doctor, who managed to save them by burning the white cankers off the children's throats and flooding them with sulfur.

The Londons next moved to Oakland, renting a comfortable five-room cottage. There Eliza, now twelve, became almost totally responsible for her little brother. If she went to school, she had to take the four-year-old along. Luckily, the other children liked him, and the teacher provided a desk and lots of picture books, which probably contributed to Jack's learning to read at an early age. During his childhood, Jack and his family moved many times, often because they could not afford to pay for the house in which they were living.

Jack Discovers the Oakland Library

During the first decade of his life, Jack had to cope with many problems, but it was not a life of constant suffering. He

An early school picture of Jack London. He is in front, third from the left. (Trust of Irving Shepard)

was not mistreated. He sometimes was hungry, but he did not starve. He enjoyed hunting and fishing with his stepfather when work allowed, and he reveled in the attention of Mammy Prentiss and Eliza. The older he grew, however, the more he was troubled by what he did not have and by circumstances he could not change. He knew that John was not his father; perhaps it did not matter.

With his mother, however, the situation was more unsettling. She seemed to pay attention to him only when it was convenient. When he was younger, she had used him as a prop in her séances, laying him on a table in a darkened room while strangers hovered over him, hoping to hear from the netherworld. She had never taken care of Jack or the house, leaving that to Mammy and Eliza. She seemed to have lost the feelings that a mother should have for her child; perhaps she never had them. This strange indifference, together with her erratic behavior and dangerous restlessness, made Jack nervous. He was growing too old for his Mammy, and Eliza had married and moved. He felt different from the other children at school. Jack was unsure of his future and confused about his past.

John London made a last attempt to provide a steady income for his family, moving to Oakland in 1886 to buy and manage a boardinghouse. It was successful, and things seemed to be going better. During this time, ten-year-old Jack made one of the great discoveries of his life: the Oakland Public Library.

Although he had been reading for at least five years, he had encountered only a handful of important books in the midst of his family's frequent moves. Most of his reading had been in newspapers and dime-store novels. Now Ina Coolbrith, the librarian, introduced him to the world of literature. He read hungrily, especially stories of adventure, travel, and discovery. He read in bed, at the table, while he walked, and during recess. He gorged himself on tales of the wide and exotic world that was just beyond the horizon.

For a while, that world remained beyond the horizon. Jack's vast appetite for literature at ten would pay richly later, because his opportunities for reading, like most of the other good things in his life, were precariously balanced. When his mother began to spend the family money foolishly, the Londons could not pay their mortgage. The bank again foreclosed on their little enterprise, and the family had to move to poorer quarters. John was now fifty-six and unable to find steady work. It was up to Jack to help the family put food on the table.

A "Work-Beast" at Eleven

Every morning Jack got up while it was still dark to deliver papers, and he threw a second route after school. The twelve dollars he earned each month went straight to Flora. He also worked weekends and nights on an ice wagon, and set pins in a bowling alley. This left him little time for reading, but it gave more opportunity for meeting the kinds of people he often had read about. The Oakland waterfront was filled with sailors who traveled—Arctic whalers, Chinese traders, Greek fishermen, and local oyster pirates. Enthralled, Jack spent time around the ships, asking for odd jobs and learning all he could about sailing. Because he was fearless in climbing the masts and rigging and was not afraid of getting wet or dirty, the yacht owners liked him and taught him how to sail.

By the time he was thirteen, Jack had managed to hoard enough nickels and dimes from the pay he gave his mother to purchase a small, leaky boat in which to hone his nautical skills. For a year, between odd jobs and paper routes, he managed to spend an hour or two almost every day in his boat. Then the all-too-familiar hammer of reality fell again. John London was seriously injured in a train accident. Jack had to go to work full time.

Jack found a full-time job in Hickmott's cannery, near the railroad tracks, working ten to eighteen hours each day stuffing pickles into jars for ten cents an hour. During the busy season he would work week after week until eleven o'clock at night, walking home because he could not afford the streetcar. He would get up in the cold darkness at half past five to wash himself with hard soap, eat a breakfast of bread and coffee, and trudge back to the cannery. What is the meaning of life, he wondered, if one is to be only a work-beast? He longed for his books and the sea.

Chapter 3

What Is a Boy, What Is a Man?

Jack's first chance to escape the hard and dreary life of a work-beast came when he was fifteen years old. An acquaintance from the Oakland waterfront, French Frank, decided to sell his small ship, the *Razzle Dazzle*. Jack wanted the sloop more than anything, so that he could become an oyster pirate. These pirates raided private oyster beds at night in order to make a quick profit. Where could he get three hundred dollars? He rushed to Mammy Prentiss to beg for the money: "Aunt Jennie, this is my only hope of escaping."

"Prince of the Oyster Pirates"

Jack met French Frank at the First and Last Chance Saloon to hand over the fifteen shiny twenty-dollar gold pieces he had been given by Aunt Jennie. After a drink of whiskey to seal the deal, Jack boarded his new prize and sailed out into San Francisco Bay. Throughout his life, sailing would be a passion and a sure release from all the problems that worried him.

As an oyster pirate, Jack made a considerable amount of money. He had to become part of a rough gang in order to do it, however, and he ran the risk of being arrested. Jack drank heavily and spent money freely when he had it. These habits, begun early, caused him many problems later in life.

After several months, Jack began to have doubts about life on the wrong side of the law. He decided to take a job which he had been offered with the California Fish Patrol. There was no salary, but he could keep half the fines he collected from

London (right), in his thirties, with French Frank, who had sold him the Razzle Dazzle *many years before.* (Trust of Irving Shepard)

those caught fishing illegally. Stationed in the old town of Benicia, just north of Oakland, Jack learned more about the waters of San Francisco Bay. He often found himself in danger as he confronted poachers or shrimpers using illegal nets.

His most dangerous experience while working with the California Fish Patrol, however, did not come at the hands of Yellow Handkerchief or any of the other fishing pirates. It came from his dangerous friend, the bottle. One night when he had been drinking heavily, Jack stumbled overboard into the fast-moving current. Fighting the riptides off Mare Island, he was picked up, gulping seawater, by a Greek fisherman four hours later. As with most of his adventures, Jack later turned this and his other experiences of almost a year with the California Fish Patrol into a book—*Tales of the Fish Patrol* (1905).

In the fall of 1892, Jack went back to Oakland, where he fell in with the hard-drinking gang of pirates and seamen who had befriended him in his oyster-raiding days. One night at a political rally he drank so much whiskey that he almost died. "I often think that was the nearest to death I have ever been," he later wrote: "I was scorching up, burning alive internally, in

24

an agony of fire and suffocation, and I wanted air—I madly wanted air." His two near brushes with death at the hands of alcohol forced to his mind all the bums and loafers he had known on the waterfront, and caused him to rethink his heavy drinking. Yet in Oakland the rough life was all he knew.

Life, Death, and the *Sophia Sutherland*

During the winter of 1892, Jack became friendly with some of the seal hunters who were wintering in San Francisco. Through them he finally got the chance to sign on as a sailor with a three-masted schooner, the *Sophia Sutherland*. It was bound for the northern Pacific Ocean on a sealing expedition. Just a few days after his seventeenth birthday he finally sailed from San Francisco Bay out into the Pacific, looking back from the other side of the Golden Gate. His soul longed for adventure.

His first few weeks aboard the *Sophia Sutherland* were the hardest. He was a good seaman and a hard worker, but he had never sailed the open seas before. All his shipmates were experienced and resented the fact that he had been brought aboard as their equal. Jack was determined to prove himself. He never left a job undone, was always the last to go below deck, and never accepted any abuse from anyone. Within a few weeks, his skill and determination won him a kind of rough equality with men who had far greater experience.

During a hundred days of sealing along the northern coasts of Japan and Manchuria, a typhoon struck the waters in which the *Sophia Sutherland* was sailing. For most of the night all hands were on deck, fighting the huge waves that caused the schooner to roll, first to starboard, then to port. At any moment she might have been broadsided by an avalanche of water. In the morning, Jack took the wheel and for forty minutes guided the hundred tons of wood and iron through the foamy waves while his exhausted shipmates finally ate some breakfast. On

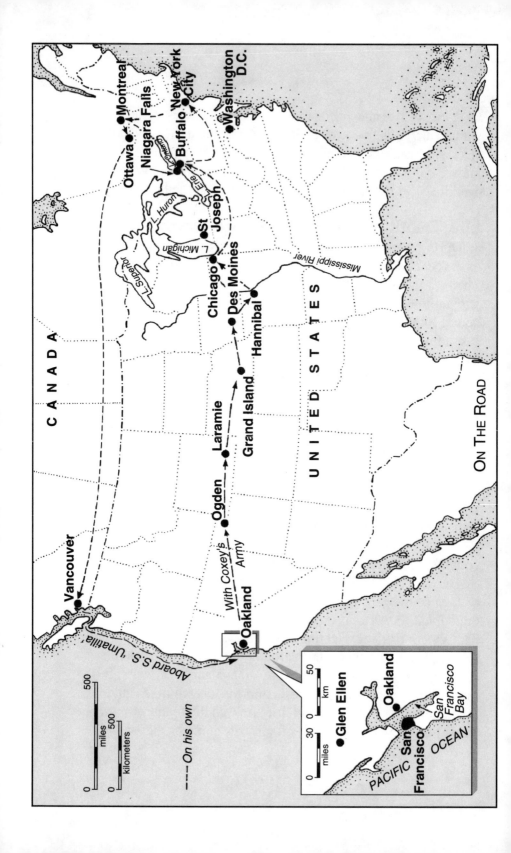

ON THE ROAD

CANADA

UNITED STATES

Vancouver

Aboard S.S. *Umatilla*

Oakland

With Coxey's Army

Ogden

Laramie

Grand Island

Hannibal

Des Moines

Chicago

St Joseph

L. Michigan

L. Superior

L. Huron

L. Erie

L. Ontario

Niagara Falls

Ottawa

Montreal

Buffalo

New York City

Washington D.C.

Mississippi River

- - - *On his own*

500
miles
0

500
kilometers
0

PACIFIC OCEAN

Glen Ellen

Oakland

San Francisco

San Francisco Bay

50
km
0

30
miles
0

August 26, 1893, the *Sophia Sutherland* slipped safely into San Francisco, and Jack headed for his home in Oakland. Eight months at sea had given him a chance to expand his nautical skills and to prove that he was more than just a coastal sailor. It also provided the material for his first published story. Although he was working ten-hour days at ten cents an hour in a jute mill after his return from sea, Jack decided to enter a descriptive writing contest sponsored by the *San Francisco Morning Call*. For three nights he labored over his "Story of a Typhoon off the Coast of Japan."

In November he learned that he had won the twenty-five-dollar first prize and would have his story and picture published in the paper. Although he had never gone beyond junior high school, Jack's story had been chosen over contributions of students from Stanford University and the University of California. It was a good start for a young writer, but he still had to drag himself back to the dreaded jute mill.

The Young Socialist

Long, dreary hours of work at the cannery, the jute mill, and later at a power station made Jack think of the inequality of wealth in the United States. He had talent but could find no honest work for more than a dollar a day. Across the country, more than two million people were out of work. Something had to be wrong, Jack thought. He began to read everything he could find that might help him understand the situation. Finally the time for action came.

In 1894, a businessman named Jacob Coxey decided to lead an "army" of unemployed men to Washington, D.C., to demand jobs from the government. In all parts of the country, industrial armies began to form. Jack had been looking for a reason to quit his life as a work-beast and decided to travel with the western army of "General" Charles T. Kelly. At first the trip was exciting. Jack enjoyed the enthusiastic crowds that often turned out on foot, on horses, or in wagons to meet the determined workers. However, after several weeks of riding the rails, rafting down rivers, and tramping down dusty roads, he had had enough. On the May night he arrived in Hannibal, Missouri, Jack wrote in his diary that he "went supperless to bed. Am going to pull out in the morning. I can't stand starvation."

Jack's goals were not the same as those of most in the "industrial army." Even while he was with the marchers, people noticed that he did things his own way. He was young and mainly looking for new adventures. Still, his experience with the army of the unemployed did help him to understand better the problems that workers faced in the United States.

From Hannibal he rode the rails, stealing and begging food. He first went to Chicago, then to New York City for a week of sightseeing. From there he pushed on to Niagara Falls. He was so captivated by the sight of the falls that he refused to take time out for supper. After a balmy night sleeping in a field, he walked into the town to find breakfast. He was promptly arrested by a policeman who was rounding up hoboes. Jack was given a fifteen-second trial and immediately sent to the Erie County Penitentiary in Buffalo for thirty days.

A month in jail taught Jack much about the realities of justice—and injustice. As he beat his way home, hoboing through Pittsburgh, Washington, D.C., New York City, and by rail across Canada, he learned from fellow travelers about the ideas of Karl Marx and socialism. There really was a huge gap between the poor and the rich that no amount of hard work could overcome. He determined that he must find a way to live by brain power, rather than by muscle power. He decided that a degree was the answer and that he must go to college.

Back to School

The problem was that Jack was not prepared. He was

At age seventeen, London sailed to Japan as an "able-bodied seaman" on the
Sophia Sutherland. (Trust of Irving Shepard)

nineteen years old but had never attended high school. Determined to make up for lost time, he entered Oakland High School with students much younger than he was. However, he soon became impatient with the teaching and with the sheltered lives of his classmates. Most had never been farther than San Francisco. He decided to quit after one year and to prepare himself with his own reading schedule.

For twelve weeks, Jack studied every day for nineteen hours. After three days of examinations at the University of California, Berkeley, in August, 1896, he applied his usual wind-and-water remedy to clear his mind. While waiting for the test scores, he went sailing for almost a week. He knew that he had passed, and in the fall of 1896 he became a "university man."

Jack found the teaching at the university less challenging than he had hoped. He also was running short of money. Gradually he convinced himself that he could learn faster on his own. In February, 1897, Jack was forced to leave the university, still hoping to return if he could find the money. He never did go back.

During high school and college, Jack met a number of wealthy people from the San Francisco Bay area. Many of them simply rejected him as a waterfront hoodlum. Others, however, could see his potential. Because Jack was witty, had seen much of the world, and was a good speaker, he was well received by the prosperous members of the Henry Clay debating club. Among them was Ted Applegarth, who introduced him to a more cultured way of life. Jack eventually found his first love in Mabel Applegarth, Ted's sister; he traveled with their family and learned to appreciate fine music.

Because Jack was both talented and poor, he never felt totally comfortable in the company of those who were a part of respectable society. Most of these people had started out in life wearing nice clothes and attending good schools. Jack went quickly back and forth between the self-confidence that his ability gave him and the shyness that his poverty forced upon him.

"Arise, Ye Americans"

Jack's poverty and his experiences on the road, at sea, and in the factories of Oakland led him to believe that there was too little justice for working people. He had become interested in socialism as a road toward a better society when he read Karl Marx's *Communist Manifesto* while on the road with Coxey's Army. During high school he wrote articles on socialism for the school newspaper, *The Aegis*. In his last article, "Optimism, Pessimism and Patriotism," Jack accused the government of allowing a system that took advantage of workers through long hours and low wages. His final sentence sounded very much like Karl Marx himself: "Arise, ye Americans, patriots and optimists! Awake! Seize the reins of a corrupted government and educate your masses!"

Even before entering the university, Jack had become well known as the "boy socialist" of the San Francisco Bay area. After leaving college, he wrote and lectured more than ever. He became famous as a member of the Oakland chapter of the Socialist Labor Party by challenging a city ordinance which made it unlawful to take part in a public meeting in certain parts of the city without the permission of the mayor. Jack drew a large crowd with a speech on the anniversary of Abraham Lincoln's birthday and was promptly arrested. Serving as his own lawyer, he convinced the judge to let him go.

Jack continued to write and lecture, but neither brought him any income. He had to return once more to the life of the work-beast, this time starching clothes in a laundry south of San Francisco for thirty dollars a month. Every time he tried to read, he fell asleep. He never managed to complete a single book while working there. When the laundry closed in June, 1897, Jack gladly packed his bags and returned home to Oakland. He was determined somehow to break out of his life of poverty and monotony.

Chapter 4

Paper Gold in the Klondike

Like dozens of ships did every week, the S.S. *Excelsior* docked in San Francisco on July 14, 1897. This one, however, was unlike any of the others. Aboard was a group of miners who had been hard at work in the Klondike region of Canada, near the Alaskan border. They brought gold from the riverbeds, and with it a kind of fever which spread throughout the United States. Men quit their jobs, abandoned their responsibilities, and borrowed other people's money in order to have a chance of striking it rich. The newspapers called it "Klondicitis," and Jack caught it.

It was not necessary for Jack to quit his job, for he did not have one. Borrowing money from his stepsister Eliza, he bought fur-lined coats and caps, boots, mittens, warm underwear, tents, blankets, and stoves. The single most important item he carried, however, was Miner Bruce's book, *Alaska*, which told him what to pack, where to go, and exactly what to do in order to stake a claim. Jack's supplies weighed almost 2,000 pounds.

Heading North

On July 25, the S.S. *Umatilla* headed for the golden north with Jack and almost five hundred other anxious prospectors aboard. They transferred to the *City of Topeka* at Port Townsend, Washington, arriving on August 2 in Juneau, Alaska, where the coastal vessels had to stop. From there they hired local Indians to paddle them a hundred miles in seventy-foot canoes to the small port of Dyea. All along the way Jack enjoyed the mountains, glaciers, and waterfalls

33

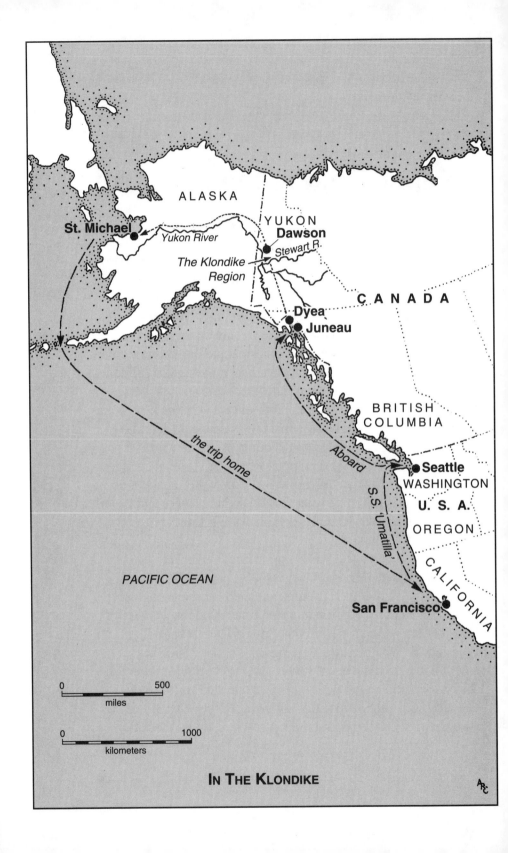

ALASKA

YUKON

Dawson

St. Michael

Yukon River

Stewart R.

The Klondike
Region

Dyea

Juneau

CANADA

BRITISH
COLUMBIA

the trip home

Aboard

S.S. 'Umatilla'

Seattle

WASHINGTON

U. S. A.

OREGON

CALIFORNIA

PACIFIC OCEAN

San Francisco

0   500
miles

0   1000
kilometers

IN THE KLONDIKE

ARC

which presented themselves on either side of the small arm of water. A few days later, Jack was put ashore at the mouth of the Dyea River.

Everything in Dyea was confused. The river had thirty-foot tides and no wharves. Every miner was trying to hire someone to help get his crates and bundles to shore. Tempers flared. Once ashore, the tents and supplies of more than fifteen hundred gold miners were scattered carelessly along the landscape. Jack was anxious to get away from the confusion.

In the race for the gold fields, everyone first had to sail six miles of the Dyea River, hike six miles up a canyon, then climb three-quarters of a mile over Chilcoot Pass. Rates for carrying loads across the pass had rocketed with the high demand, from eight to forty cents a pound—far beyond Jack's ability to pay. As a result, he packed all his own goods, just as he had planned. The trail was rugged, but Jack joined three other prospectors to make the work easier and the journey more pleasant.

Hiking up the canyon, the would-be miners had to ford the icy Dyea River many times. Sometimes they lashed logs together to form footbridges that were quite unsteady for men with hundred-pound packs. Often they fell into the freezing waters, delaying their progress to dry out and rearrange their loads.

Sheep Camp was the point of no return, the place where men searched their souls. They either strengthened their determination or gave up in despair. As they climbed above the timber line there was no wood for fires, and the boulders became larger and more difficult to travel over. Men and animals suffered terribly. Jack hated to see delirious prospectors furiously whip their horses, urging them on. Sometimes they beat them to death with hammers. Jack told a friend that if all the dead horses and mules along the trail were laid side by side, a man could walk fifty miles on horseflesh.

When they reached the Scales, a place where loads were once again weighed, Chilcoot Pass loomed almost straight up above them. Trip after trip after trip, Jack struggled up with loads weighing anywhere from 75 to 150 pounds. Then he would scramble back down the steep incline to reload for another trip to the top. On September 8, one month after leaving Dyea with his first load, he finally reached Lake Linderman, just beyond the pass.

Running the Rapids

Once over Chilcoot Pass, the going was easier because they could often travel on the rivers. The race now was against the approaching northern winter. Immediately Jack and his friends set up a boat-building site by a patch of spruce trees. Together, seven men built two boats, the *Yukon Belle* and the *Belle of the Yukon*, in only two weeks. They had to be well built, for ahead lay five hundred miles of rivers, with more than their share of both calm lakes and raging rapids.

Normally men would unload their boats and haul them with a line when navigating an especially rapid stream. Jack and his friends decided, however, that the winter freeze was too near to take the time. Although many boats had been wrecked and many men drowned trying to steer them loaded through treacherous waters, they took their chances. Jack had never

London carved his name into the wood of his Yukon cabin, identifying himself as "miner, author." (Trust of Irving Shepard)

sailed boats like these, but he knew how wind and currents affected a craft and was confident that he could get them through.

The most dangerous passage was on the Fifty Mile River, where it flowed out of Marsh Lake. In some places it was more than four hundred yards wide. As the flowing water approached Box Canyon, however, it narrowed to a hundred yards, made a great bend, then shot through towering rock walls only eighty feet apart. The sudden contraction of the river created an unusual ridge of water, six to eight feet high, in the middle of the river.

When Jack and his friends arrived, hundreds of miners were portaging their supplies. Jack's party had to decide whether to unload the boats or try and navigate the treacherous river with the boats full. Two days of risk-free, backbreaking work, or the most exciting and dangerous two-minute journey of their lives—that was the choice. Jack was through with the life of the work-beast. They all decided to go through and take their chances.

With miners lining the river banks, Jack and his comrades began to pick up speed as the river narrowed. "Be sure to keep on the ridge," men on the bank yelled. At first they did, but the *Yukon Belle* was overloaded and soon slipped off, veering dangerously to within a few feet of the rock walls. Jack leaned against the steering oar with all his might and managed to turn the boat toward the center of the current. Almost miraculously they mounted the ridge again.

Their amazing success at Box Canyon led Jack's party to take other chances. As a result, they were far ahead of most of the miners who had docked at Dyea in August. On October 9 they tied up at Split-Up Island, between the Stewart River and Henderson Creek. There they found an abandoned cabin and decided to wait out the long Yukon winter, preparing themselves to become rich in the spring.

Camp Life

Signs of failure were all around. Many people already were heading home, discouraged by the hard life and the prospects of a famine because so many miners had crowded in. Jack knew that he and his friends had to do two things immediately.

First, they had to make the old cabin a fit place to live during the long winter. Jack also realized that most of the streams and rivers had already been claimed. He decided that

Books Important to Jack London

Signa *(1875), by Ouida (Marie de la Ramee).*
A melodramatic novel about the illegitimate son of an Italian peasant girl who becomes one of Italy's most famous composers. London read it many times during his youth, perhaps first around 1884.
The Communist Manifesto *(1848), by Karl Marx.*
The famous pamphlet which first attracted London to socialism. Jack read it in 1895 after his journey with Coxey's army and a week in the penitentiary.
Paradise Lost *(1667), by John Milton.*
Considered the greatest epic poem in English; Milton gives a poetic account of Satan's attack on the paradise of Eden.
On the Origin of Species *(1859), by Charles Darwin.*
Darwin's explanation of his theory of evolution. This book popularized the theory of "survival of the fittest" so common in London's own work.
First Principles *(1862), by Herbert Spencer.*
London said that Spencer attempted to relate all things to one another, "from the farthermost star in the wastes of space to the myriads of atoms in the grains of sand under one's foot." He thought this book had "done more for mankind" than a thousand popular novels.
Psychology of the Unconscious *(1916, English translation), by Carl Jung.*
A pioneering work that led to London's increased interest in psychology in his later works. London's copy contains 300 notations, more than any other book in his library.

his only chance of finding gold was on Henderson Creek, the only unstaked area left in the Yukon. For three days, Jack and his friends explored Henderson Creek, returning with eight claims. After recording their claims in Dawson, eighty miles to the north, they returned in December to their cabin on Split-Up Island to wait out the winter.

There was much work to do just to survive. Wood always needed to be chopped and split. Ice had to be cut and melted for drinking water. When the weather was good, Jack would travel the eighteen miles to his cabin on Henderson Creek to work his claim. It was too cold and frozen, however, for him to do any serious mining. Cabin floors were so cold that food stored there would not thaw. As a result, Jack spent many hours in his bunk reading. When every pound made a difference in packing into the Yukon, Jack still chose to carry Charles Darwin's *On the Origin of Species*, Herbert Spencer's *Philosophy of Style*, Karl Marx's *Capital*, and John Milton's *Paradise Lost* over Chilcoot Pass.

Jack did not hide himself away to read and study, however. He frequently sat around fires in various cabins on Split-Up Island, talking about socialism and learning all he could from experienced prospectors. One of Jack's Yukon friends, Emil Jensen, remembered that Jack always stood ready "to undertake a two days' hike for a plug of tobacco when he saw us restless and grumpy for want of a smoke."

Jack enjoyed each moment's activity for itself instead of thinking only about how it might help him in the future. This was one thing that made him so different from most people. Nevertheless, those frozen months on Split-Up Island were a turning point in his life. He listened to the tales of the old-timers; he talked to gamblers in Dawson and trappers who had known the region long before "Klondicitis" took over. He took mental notes. Little by little the characters of his future books were being formed. Burning Daylight, the Malemute

The cabin in which Jack lived while in the Yukon. (Trust of Irving Shepard)

Kid, Yellow Legs, and a pack of dogs and wolves were being born, but only Jack London knew it.

Drifting Back to Earth

There were few fruits or vegetables available in the Klondike. Most of the men lived on beans, bread, and bacon. As a result, in May, 1898, Jack developed a serious case of scurvy. His face was covered with sores, and his gums were swollen and bleeding. It was impossible for him to work his claim. He could not get better without medical attention, so Jack and Dr. Harvey, a fellow prospector, tore down their cabin to build a raft that would take them to Dawson. There they sold the logs for six hundred dollars so Jack could buy food and medicine. It was not enough, however. He had to go home to recover.

On June 8, 1898, Jack began the nineteen-hundred-mile journey down the Yukon River from Dawson to the Bering

Sea. The Yukon was a broad highway, and the trip was uneventful. Jack began to keep a diary. On June 18 he wrote that the "few raw potatoes and tomatoes" he was given in Anvik were "worth more to me at the present stage of the game than an El Dorado claim." Already he was thinking about which stories he could sell to the magazines.

Although Jack left the Klondike thinking he might return, he never did. There was little gold in his claim, which he probably realized before he left. Still, he later recalled that "it was in the Klondike that I found myself. There you get your perspective." He had experienced a great adventure, which he always enjoyed. He had tested himself against the winter, just as earlier he had tested himself against the toughs on the Oakland waterfront and against the sea on the *Sophia Sutherland*. In each case he had experienced hard knocks but had come out ahead. It was clear to Jack that he must write. Now he had something to write about.

Chapter 5

The Literary Lion

Jack arrived in Oakland late in July to find that his father had died the previous October. As head of the family, he was expected to provide for his mother Flora and little Johnny Miller, his stepsister Ida's son, whom his mother was now raising. Although Jack desperately wanted to write, the financial demands were urgent, so he went to look for work.

Head of the House

His skills were useful only on a ship and in a laundry. Going to sea was out of the question under the circumstances, and not a single laundry was hiring. The west coast of the United States was still suffering from an economic depression that had struck in 1893. Work was very hard to find.

In order to pay the rent and put food on the table, Jack had to pawn his few possessions. His watch, his bicycle, and his father's mackintosh all had to go. Later he pawned his remaining gold dust and mining supplies, giving up the slim chance of returning to the Klondike.

Jack tried to write his way out his desperate circumstances. If he could not find steady work, at least he could do what he enjoyed to earn some money. He sent an article, "From Dawson to the Sea," to the *San Francisco Bulletin*. The editor returned the story, with a note penciled across the bottom. He could not buy it, he said, because interest in Alaska had "subsided in an amazing degree." This was the first of forty-four rejections that Jack would receive by the end of the year.

For months Jack wrote manuscripts and mailed them. He

tried short stories, poetry, essays, ballads, and songs. He wrote about light-hearted matters and serious concerns. No one was buying. The regular trek to the mailbox was a little like moving goods up Chilcoot Pass, going up loaded and coming back empty. The only trouble was that he had nothing to show for it.

Jack knew that he had talent, but he did not know anyone in the publishing business. He had to learn everything on his own. During September he saw an advertisement for a postal job. It would not be very exciting work, but he knew that sixty-five dollars a month would give him a secure financial base. On October 1, he took the exam for the job. Although he did not know it at the time, he had the highest score, and the post office was simply waiting for an opening before making Jack an offer.

Toward the end of November, Jack received a thin letter from the *Overland Monthly Magazine,* to whom he had submitted a short story, "To the Man on the Trail." The size of the letter was a good sign; obviously there was no returned manuscript inside. He was thrilled as he scanned the letter. "We have read your manuscript and are so greatly pleased with it," it began. However, his joy departed as he continued to read: "We will publish it in the January number if you can content yourself with five dollars." Jack was devastated. An article in a local newspaper had led him to believe that the minimum pay for writing was ten dollars per thousand words. At that rate he should have received at least forty dollars! What should he do?

By one of life's strange coincidences, after weeks of receiving nothing but rejection slips, another thin envelope was delivered that afternoon. In it was a letter from H. D. Umbstaetter of *The Black Cat.* At four thousand words, Jack's story "A Thousand Deaths" was more "lengthy than strengthy," he wrote, but if Jack would cut it in half, he would

43

London enjoyed writing outdoors; here he is working near Wake Robin Lodge in California. (Trust of Irving Shepard)

be pleased to send a check for forty dollars. Forty dollars for two thousand words was twice the rate Jack was expecting. Years later London confessed that it was *The Black Cat* story that "kept him in the writing game."

Security in the Mail

With the forty dollars he received for "A Thousand Deaths," Jack paid two months' rent as well as the grocer and butcher bills. He stocked the house with food, bought a winter suit, and got his bicycle, watch, and mackintosh out of hock. Finally, he bought typing paper and pencils. When he counted his money, he found only two dollars left—just enough for stamps to keep his writing in the mail for another few weeks.

On January 16, 1899, Jack heard that he was first on the post office list and would probably receive a call to work in April. Should he take the secure job, earning twice as much as he ever had, or should he continue to write? His mother urged him to pursue his dream. Although she had never taken much time with Jack, she believed in his ability. She was willing to continue, for a few more months or years, giving piano lessons and living hand-to-mouth. It was probably the biggest sacrifice she ever made for him.

Jack's writing did not immediately make him famous. He wrote sixty-one new items for submission in 1899. These, along with the dozens which had already been rejected in 1898, were in constant circulation to editors around the country. "The Story of Keesh" was rejected twenty-four times before it was finally published in 1904. Never again would he receive so many rejection slips—266—as he did in 1899.

One editor rejected a London story as "too tragic." He said that *Vogue* magazine wanted "little love stories of 1,600 words." Another editor turned down a story as "absolutely impossible" for his magazine: "We want clean, happy stories of love or incident." Unfortunately for Jack in 1899, he could not write that kind of story, for he had personally experienced the harsh realities which most people in the United States faced.

Nevertheless, Jack had some successes. His short stories of the frozen northland began to sell. One of the finest, "The White Silence," had been written the year before and rejected twice before being accepted for publication by the *Overland Monthly* in January. They also published his "In a Far Country" in June. Also in June, *The Illustrated Buffalo Express* published "From Dawson to the Sea." He was not yet making much money publishing in these smaller magazines and newspapers, but he was beginning to be read from coast to coast. Jack had long been convinced that if he could just get people to read his material, they would demand more of it.

His big break came on October 30, when the famous magazine *Atlantic Monthly* sent him a check for $120 for his story "An Odyssey of the North." He rushed to tell Flora. "Mother, look! Look! I did it! . . . All the Eastern editors will see it. They'll want to buy too. We're on our way up!" Once again he paid bills and got his things back from the pawn shop. He was anxious to see how the public would respond when his story was published in the first month of a new century.

Financially, Jack had not done very well during 1899. His average monthly earnings were less than he had made at the laundry. On the other hand, he liked the work better, and he had finally had a story accepted by a famous magazine. He had learned much and had at least made ends meet. Things looked promising for the future.

A New Century, a New Life

"An Odyssey of the North" was shocking to many readers accustomed to the sugar-coated literature that most major magazines published during the 1890's. Many editors had rejected it because of its violent and harsh passages. However, there was a new generation of readers that these editors did not yet understand. As public education reached more and more working people, they joined the reading public. These readers wanted stories about real people struggling with nature and society.

Jack London had grown up struggling. He never had a stable home life, and he often went hungry. He knew what it was like to work hard, to sleep outside, and to be unable to find a job. Jack had lived through troubles that many people in the United States faced. Yet he also had experienced adventures that most readers only dreamed of. This combination of everyday hardship and adventurous escape made his stories very popular. Jack's work was, in his own words, realism fused "with the fancies and beauties of imagination." He wanted to show life "as it was, with all its spirit-groping and soul-reaching left in."

During 1900, Jack became well known and finally began to earn a substantial amount of money—more than twenty-five

Newlyweds Jack and Bessie London go on a bicycle excursion. (Trust of Irving Shepard)

hundred dollars for the year. He published numerous articles as well as his first book, a collection of short stories about the Yukon entitled *The Son of the Wolf.* One critic praised him by saying that he "drew a vivid picture of the cold, darkness, and starvation, the pleasures of human companionship in adverse circumstances, and the sterling qualities which the rough battle with nature brings out." London was regarded as one of the most promising writers in the United States.

On April 7, 1900, he married the slender and athletic Bessie Maddern. Her fiancé, who had been Jack's friend, had died during the Spanish-American War. Jack made it clear that he did not love Bessie, but he liked her and admired her skills and independence. He was convinced by his studies that love really did not exist, that men and women should simply be companions in the pursuit of common goals.

During the next two years, Jack's star rose rapidly. After publication of *The Son of the Wolf,* critics began to call him the "Kipling of the North." Just as Rudyard Kipling, the English author, wrote exotic and authentic tales about adventure in India, Jack made the frozen north come alive for thousands of readers. Jack was very pleased with this compliment, because Kipling had long been a hero to him.

Although his first novel, *A Daughter of the Snows,* was not successful, his stories continued to sell for high prices. Yet Jack always seemed to be in debt. The more famous he became, the more he liked to entertain friends, which was an expensive hobby. Within a year of his marriage, he also began making payments for two houses. One was for Bessie, himself, and their young daughter, Joan, who had been born in January, 1901. The other house he rented for his mother and Johnny Miller. When bills had to be paid, Jack would write almost anything for anybody. Once he wrote a series of ten articles for the San Francisco *Examiner* on a shooting competition.

In the summer of 1902, Jack decided to write a different

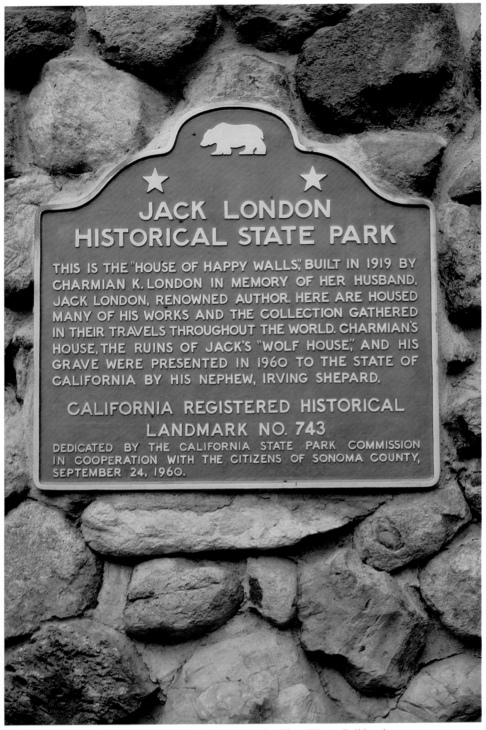

1. Descriptive plaque at the Jack London Museum in Glen Ellen, California.
(Deborah Cowder)

2. The remains of London's Wolf House, destroyed by fire in 1913 before its completion. It is now part of the Jack London Historical State Park. (Deborah Cowder)

3. The "House of Happy Walls," built by Charmian London in 1919-1922. It now houses the Jack London Museum. (Deborah Cowder)

4. The cottage on London's ranch in which Jack and Charmian lived. (Deborah Cowder)

5. The study at the London Museum contains many of Jack's possessions and books. (Deborah Cowder)

6. A model of London's yacht, the *Snark*, is displayed at the Jack London Museum.
   (Deborah Cowder)

7. Sculptures and a war drum from London's art collection, acquired during his many travels. On display at the Jack London Museum. (Deborah Cowder)

8. Jack London's Socialist Party membership cards. (Deborah Cowder)

9. A poster for the 1940 film *Queen of the Yukon*, based on a London story.
   (Deborah Cowder)

10. The cover of the Bengali translation of *The Call of the Wild*. The book has been translated into more than eighty languages. (Deborah Cowder)

11. London's *White Fang* was made into a popular film by Walt Disney Pictures in 1991. (Deborah Cowder)

12. The 1952 film *The Fighter*, based on London's story "The Mexican," is about a boxer who uses his prize money to buy arms to overthrow a dictator. (Deborah Cowder)

13. The First and Last Chance Saloon, where young Jack bought a boat from French Frank, still stands in Oakland, California. (Deborah Cowder)

14. The cabin in which London lived in the Yukon in 1897-1898 now stands in Jack London Square, Oakland, California. (Deborah Cowder)

kind of book. He went to England, where he pretended to be a stranded American sailor. He plunged into London's East End, where the most miserable and hungry people in England lived. Again, Jack was reminded of how unfair society seemed to be. He found many people who wanted to work but could not find jobs. Typically the homeless walked all night, for they were not allowed to sleep on benches or in parks. Jack wrote that he was once "out all night with homeless ones, walking the streets in the bitter rain, drenched to the skin, wondering when dawn would come."

During his three months away from the United States, Jack divided his time between living in the East End, studying books and government documents, taking photographs, traveling, and typing his book. When he returned to New York City on November 4, *People of the Abyss* was ready for the publisher. He said that more of his heart went into it than any of his other books.

He was anxious to get back to Oakland. His second daughter, Becky, had been born during October while he was away. As usual, Jack had to borrow money from his publisher, George Brett, in order to buy his train ticket home.

The Call of the Wild

Shortly after returning to Oakland, Jack wrote to Brett telling him of several books that he was either writing or would like to write. They included a collection of stories about his experiences with the California Fish Patrol, a new collection of Klondike stories, two novels, and a book of letters about love. He was already liked well enough by the reading public that Brett agreed to give him $150 per month in advance while he worked on these books.

Before completing any of the projects he had mentioned, however, Jack wanted to correct the bad impression of dogs that he thought he had given in his short story "Diable—A

Facts about *The Call of The Wild*

Published: 1903

Editions: More than 400, including a Boy Scout edition. It has
             never been out of print.

Translations: It has been translated into more than 80 languages.

Acclaim: "The Call of the Wild *is the greatest dog-story ever
            written and is at the same time a study of one of the most
            curious and profound motives that plays hide-and-seek
            in the human soul. the more civilized we become the
            deeper is the fear that back in barbarism is something
            of the beauty and joy of life we have not brought along
            with us.* "
                         Carl Sandburg (1906)

            "*. . . A story no other man could have written.* "
                         William Lyon Phelps (1916)

            "*Here indeed are all the elements of sound fiction: clear
            thinking, a sense of character, the dramatic instinct,
            and, above all, the adept putting together of words. . .* "
                         H. L. Mencken (1918)

            *This was, in a manner, Jack London's story, symboli-
            cally told—which explained why* The Call of the Wild
            *was perhaps his best book, written directly from his
            unconscious. . .* "
                         Van Wyck Brooks (1952)

Dog." The story's main character was a vicious beast. Now he wanted to tell the tale of a dog as a noble creature. What began as a short story of four thousand words got away from him and became more than eight times that length. In January, 1903, he submitted the completed manuscript of *The Call of the Wild* to *The Saturday Evening Post*. He continued writing a thousand words a day on his other projects.

Buck, the main character of *The Call of the Wild*, begins as a domestic dog that has always been kindly treated. However, Buck is stolen from his home in California by a servant, sold, and taken north into the icy Klondike. He gradually abandons his domestic habits in order to adapt to the harsh environment. Finally, Buck's natural instincts take over. In the course of hunting and fighting with a pack of wolves, he becomes their leader, totally wild and singing "the song of the pack." Jack believed that humans, like domesticated animals, were civilized only on the surface. When faced with the hard struggles of life, they too could become wild.

Jack did not know that his new novel would be one of the most famous books of all time. It became popular around the world, giving him an international reputation that he never lost. It has long been the most widely read American novel in Russia. According to one critic, it is both "the greatest dog story ever written" and an important study of the human soul. Writing *The Call of the Wild* came easily for Jack London because he, like Buck, had always struggled with life just as it was.

Chapter 6

Escape at Sea

With the success of *The Call of the Wild,* Jack now seldom received rejection slips. His books were successful with both critics and the public. *Children of the Frost,* a collection of stories published in 1902, was widely praised as worthy of Rudyard Kipling. *The Cruise of the Dazzler* (1902) and *Tales of the Fish Patrol* (1905), collections of stories for youth, brought excellent reviews. The *Kempton-Wace Letters* (1903) and *People of the Abyss* (1903) were too serious to be best-sellers, but they were praised by critics. Jack's next novel, *The Sea-Wolf,* went to number one on the best-seller list in 1904, selling forty thousand copies before publication. By 1905, Jack was recognized as a master of his craft.

Professional success does not guarantee personal happiness, however. Jack and Bessie had been happy enough as companions during their first two years of marriage. They took bicycle rides together, and she helped with the typing of manuscripts. They had the kind of unsentimental marriage that Jack argued for in the *Kempton-Wace Letters.*

In time, however, problems began to develop. She was hurt by his lack of emotion, and he was frustrated by her narrow point of view. In 1903 Jack fell in love with Charmian Kittredge. Whereas Bessie was serious and traditional, Charmian was full of fun and ready for any adventure. He wrote that he loved her "flash of spirit." That summer he left Bessie and his daughters.

For one of the few times in his life, Jack had trouble writing. There was too much on his mind. He was separated from Bessie but not yet able to be with Charmian openly. He had sold the magazine rights to *The Sea-Wolf* for four thousand dollars, but would not receive the money for several months. It was December, but he had bought no presents and had only twenty dollars.

War Correspondent

Half a world away from San Francisco, a war was brewing. Tensions had been building between Russia and Japan. When war between the two nations seemed certain, five companies bid for Jack's services in reporting the action. It was a great opportunity. He could earn some desperately needed money, have a new adventure, and get away from his personal troubles. He signed a contract with the Hearst newspapers and, on January 7, 1904, sailed for Yokohama, Japan.

No one knew exactly where the fighting might break out. The Japanese were doing all they could to keep the war correspondents in Yokohama. Jack knew that he would miss the real action if he waited there patiently, so he slipped away. When he was caught taking photographs of the fortified town of Moji, he was put in jail. After he was released, he tried time and again to find a ship going to Korea, where he suspected the fighting would start. Each time, the Japanese government stopped the vessel before it reached its destination.

Determined, Jack hired a small ship called a junk to take him to Korea. He made it, but the ship was too badly damaged to continue. This time an open boat called a sampan was found. For eight days in February he sailed along the southern and western coasts of Korea. There were raging storms, and the temperature often fell below zero. The only heat came from a small charcoal box which held a half dozen faintly glowing embers.

When he finally arrived in Chemulpo, the major port of Korea, he was greeted by R. L. Dunn, a correspondent who had gone straight to Korea instead of stopping first in

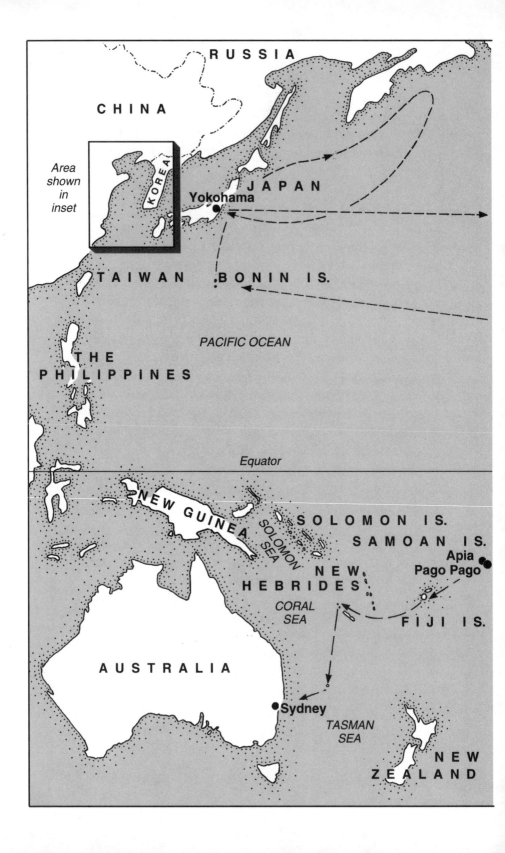

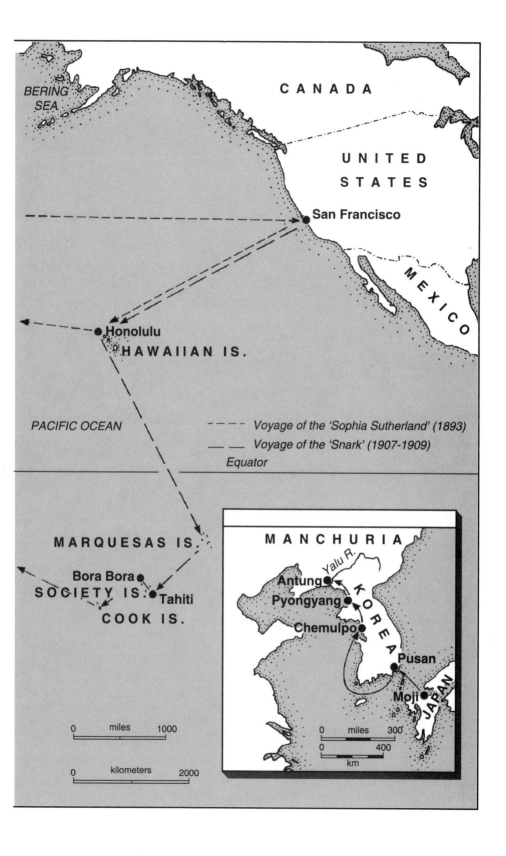

BERING
SEA

C A N A D A

U N I T E D
S T A T E S

San Francisco

M
E
X
I
C
O

Honolulu
H A W A I I A N   I S .

PACIFIC OCEAN

– – – – Voyage of the 'Sophia Sutherland' (1893)

— — Voyage of the 'Snark' (1907-1909)

Equator

M A R Q U E S A S   I S .

Bora Bora
S O C I E T Y   I S .
Tahiti
C O O K   I S .

M A N C H U R I A

Yalu R.

Antung
Pyongyang
Chemulpo

K O R E A

Pusan

Moji

J A P A N

| 0 | miles | 1000 |

| 0 | kilometers | 2000 |

0	miles	300
0	400	
km		

R. L. Dunn's photograph of London in Korea; Dunn said that London was writing while "crouched in a filthy hut, half frozen." (Trust of Irving Shepard)

Yokohama. Dunn described Jack as "a physical wreck. His ears were frozen; his fingers were frozen; his feet were frozen." Jack did not seem to mind. He had been sent to report the war, and he was determined to do it.

Jack and Dunn traveled across the mountainous and icy

72

terrain on the way to Manchuria. They often slept on the frozen ground and wondered if the nights would ever end. Many times they were detained by the Japanese for trying to get too close to the fighting. The closest they ever came was five miles, when a Japanese general put them on a high bluff overlooking the Battle of the Yalu. They were so far away that they could not even hear the noise of the guns.

Jack was bitterly disappointed and disgusted with all the restrictions. He had done his best, sending nineteen articles and many photographs to the San Francisco *Examiner*. He did not realize until he returned to California in June that he had gotten more articles out of Korea than any other correspondent. The *Examiner* had given them enormous headlines. This, combined with the popularity of *The Call of the Wild* and advance publicity for *The Sea-Wolf*, added to Jack's growing worldwide fame.

Marrying the "Mate-woman"

Before Jack could even set foot on land, he was notified by authorities that Bessie had filed for divorce. In November, 1904, the divorce became final. After a one-year waiting period, Jack would be free to remarry. He was unhappy that so many people were being hurt by the divorce, but he was convinced that it was the right thing to do. With four thousand dollars from his war work and advanced payments for *The Sea-Wolf*, he built Bessie and his girls a comfortable house in Oakland. Jack and Bessie never got along after the divorce. Still, he saw to it that his family was comfortable.

During the year that Jack was waiting for the divorce to become final, he was daily becoming more famous. His books were the talk of the literary world. He was also becoming infamous around San Francisco Bay. In February, 1905, he accepted the Socialist Party's nomination for mayor of Oakland. There was no chance that a socialist would actually be elected, but the speeches provided good publicity for their cause.

Many people had at first believed that Jack's socialism was only a hobby. After the campaign they knew differently. He delivered powerful speeches denouncing economic injustice. During the campaign, his collection of revolutionary articles, *War of the Classes*, was published. The social set of the Bay area turned against him. Book sales began to drop. Still, Jack believed deeply in the need to change the economic system of the United States and was willing to take risks for that belief.

During the summer of 1905, Jack and Charmian got to know each other better. They were both living in the small town of Glen Ellen, north of San Francisco. In the mornings he would write his thousand words a day and answer mail, while she would type. In the afternoons they rode horses, boxed, swam, and visited local sites.

Jack (left) and Charmian in 1909, with friend Frank Strawn-Hamilton. (Trust of Irving Shepard)

They also searched for a place to live. Jack had never been comfortable in Oakland society. He loved Glen Ellen and could write just as easily there. In June they visited a tract of land covered by a wilderness of shrubs and trees. Later that month Jack purchased the first tract of what would become the Jack London Ranch. He was devoted to the ranch and spent tens of thousands of dollars during his life to improve it.

Jack and Charmian were married in November, 1905, and remained happily married until the end of Jack's life. In some ways they were an unusual couple. Charmian was well educated and was more than five years older than Jack. However, in important ways they were similar. Both were unconventional and loved adventures. Neither cared for what other people thought or said. Jack built his life around writing, and Charmian enjoyed helping him type and edit.

Most important, they were deeply in love with each other. From the time of their first romance in 1903, Jack referred to Charmian as his "mate-woman," someone who understood his deepest thoughts and desires. For instance, when he suggested that someday after they had built a house they might sail around the world, Charmian asked why they should wait. "I love a boat," she said. "You love a boat; let's call the boat our house until we get ready to stay a little while in one place." This was the adventuresome spirit that Jack adored.

The Voyage of the *Snark*

That conversation of 1905 was the beginning of one of the great adventures of Jack's life. Early in 1906 he paid a shipbuilder a thousand dollars as a down payment for building a forty-three-foot yacht, which he named the *Snark*. Construction was delayed because of the great San Francisco earthquake and fire of August 18. After that, materials for the boat were expensive and hard to find. Jack planned to spend seven thousand dollars building the *Snark*, but in the end the ship cost him thirty thousand dollars.

The delays and expense were distracting, but Jack and Charmian were determined to have just the yacht they wanted. There was no question of reconsidering the voyage, for they both loved sailing and wanted to see the world. Jack had also already promised stories of the voyage to many of the best magazines in the country, including *Cosmopolitan, Collier's,* and *Woman's Home Companion.* Finally, after endless delays, the *Snark* sailed on April 23, 1907. Work on the *Snark* was still not completed, but Jack had decided to finish it in Hawaii.

Thousands of fans and friends lined the docks to watch the Londons embark on their voyage. The first leg of the journey, from San Francisco to Honolulu, was a disaster. The hull leaked, ruining tools and a three-month food supply. The main engine was not working, nor were the captain and crew very reliable. In Hawaii Jack had to replace the captain and two crew members. Jack learned how to navigate at sea and managed to steer the seeping *Snark* into Hawaiian waters. On May 20, they sighted Makapuu Point and sailed around Diamond Head into full view of Honolulu.

The five months spent in Hawaii were enjoyable. Jack was famous, and people were anxious to entertain him and Charmian. There were many beautiful and interesting sights to see, including the fiery Kilauea volcano. He also had time to write. In a little cottage near Pearl Harbor, under tropical skies, he wrote several stories, including one of his most famous tales of the frozen north, "To Build a Fire." With the *Snark* finally in good repair, the new crew, with Jack as captain, pushed her out of Pearl Harbor for the two-thousand-mile voyage to the Marquesas Islands.

From October 7 until December 6, the sea world was all the voyagers on the *Snark* knew. They saw no vessels of any kind for two months. The passage was difficult, for the winds did not blow exactly in the direction needed. Sometimes they

London at the helm of the Snark, *taking it on its first trial run.* (Trust of Irving Shepard)

would lie in the water becalmed for two days at a time. For nine weeks, fishing and working became the daily routine for the sailors. The sudden storms, the catching of a sea turtle or shark, and the bursts of precious sea breeze were all a welcome relief from the distractions and reporters that usually plagued the famous writer.

For the next year, the *Snark* carried its crew to many famous Pacific sites. In December they landed in the Marquesas Islands, which as a boy Jack had read about in Herman Melville's novel *Typee*. Later that month they reached Tahiti, where the *Snark*'s engine was finally repaired and Jack finished his autobiographical novel *Martin Eden*. The ten April days in 1908 that they spent in Bora Bora were the happiest of the trip. The crew was

Jack and Charmian London on Hawaii's Waikiki Beach. (Trust of Irving Shepard)

treated to a round of festivals and loaded with gifts.

From there, Jack sailed to Samoa, where he saw the home of one of his favorite authors, the Scotsman Robert Louis Stevenson. In the Solomon Islands, someone in the crew was almost always sick. Malaria was the most common illness. There were few fruits and vegetables to eat. Many in the crew developed the yaws, a tropical disease which caused open sores, and ngari-ngari, a rash which caused severe itching. All of these could be cured. However, when Jack's hands began to swell, he started to worry. His skin peeled, and the new skin grew back hard and thick. He feared that he had contracted leprosy while in Hawaii, and he knew that there was no cure for it. The only way to be sure was to go to Australia, where he could consult with medical experts.

In mid-November, 1908, Jack and Charmian arrived in Sydney, Australia, on the steamer *Makambo*. They had left the *Snark* in Penduffryn in the Solomon Islands, awaiting their return. The doctors informed Jack that he had a severe case of psoriasis and should return to the healthy climate of California. He and Charmian were heartbroken that they could not continue their voyage.

Within a few months, Jack was completely healthy again. He had not been able to see the Yangtze River in China, or to sail the Mediterranean Sea, as he had hoped, but he and Charmian had enjoyed a great adventure. They had made the *Snark* their mobile home for eighteen months. Although he did not complete his voyage around the world, he did not disappoint his readers. He had many tales to tell. After arriving in California in July, 1909, and telling people of all the hardships they had endured, Jack found it hard to convince them that the whole voyage was done simply "for the fun of it."

Chapter 7

The London Way of Life

Shortly before he had been forced to abandon the voyage of the *Snark*, Jack informed his publisher that he had completed five books—*Lost Face, Revolution and Other Essays, When God Laughs, South Sea Tales*, and *The Cruise of the "Snark."* He needed the money, for he returned from his twenty-seven-month absence to find that he was deeply in debt.

The Steady Workman

The *Snark* had been a great financial drain. Keeping up the Jack London Ranch was also expensive, especially because money had been wasted while he was away. Jack was thrilled that his manager had purchased two adjoining pieces of land that enlarged the ranch to 390 acres. Still, it had cost money that he had to pay back. Out of both necessity and habit, Jack relentlessly kept up his thousand words a day, with very few misses.

The steady production of stories, novels, and newspaper articles led to the most common criticism of Jack London as a writer: that he turned out too many "half-done books." He always said that he wrote to live, rather than living to write. He enjoyed sailing, ranching, and entertaining friends. Writing—even writing half-done books or articles—was the only way he knew to earn enough money to do all the things he loved and still support those who depended on him.

Building an Estate

After the voyage of the *Snark*, developing the ranch became Jack's priority. He had purchased the first piece of land as a way to enjoy the country and solitude, but as the ranch grew he wanted it to become profitable. By 1910 he had added the seven-hundred-acre Kohler-Frohling Tokay Ranch. Before his death he would add almost four hundred more acres, making his ranch one of the largest in the Valley of the Moon, the area of California in which it was located.

Agricultural experts regarded Jack as "one of California's leading farmers." He practiced terracing and drainage on his ranch, which was unusual in those days. He experimented with new crops and with seed that was best suited to the soil and climate of the area. His "pig palace" was considered the ideal in clean living for hogs, and his concrete-block silo was the first in California. When he needed more water for irrigation he built a dam on the side of a mountain, then stocked the lake with catfish.

Jack and Charmian in California after their return from their Snark *adventures.* (Trust of Irving Shepard)

Because much of the land was unsuitable for farming or grazing, he made a careful study of other uses to which it might be put. Early in 1910 he ordered fifteen thousand eucalyptus trees, which promoters promised would grow well and produce marketable timber in the rough country forty miles north of Oakland. He eventually planted 140,000 trees. Jack was unlucky with the eucalyptus, for they proved to be worthless. However, by paying careful attention to the special needs of his ranching and farming operations, he produced large crops of prunes, grapes, and alfalfa on land that had been considered unfit by previous owners. His livestock also won many prizes in county and state fairs.

Jack was often criticized for his "experiments" in agriculture. Some paid off, others did not. Yet, as he argued, he "earned his money honestly," rather than from the labor of others. He asked, "If I want to spend it to give employment, to rehabilitate California ranching, why have I not the right to spend my money for my own peculiar kind of enjoyment?" He was always free with his money in a good cause, and he instructed his ranch manager never to turn away anyone looking for work until he had three or four days' pay and three or four square meals.

Wolf House

Shortly after their marriage, Jack and Charmian planned their dream house, although work did not begin until 1911. Wolf House was planned to reflect Jack's lifestyle and sense of beauty. The main building materials were redwood trees with bark still attached, volcanic stones, blue slate, and boulders. His workroom was a nineteen-foot by forty-foot room on the third floor, connected by a spiral staircase to a library of the same size below it. The living room was eighteen by fifty-eight feet, two stories high, with a huge stone fireplace.

Jack had always loved to entertain. He wanted his new

London on his ranch with one of his beloved horses, the stallion Neuadd Hillside. (Trust of Irving Shepard)

home to have plenty of room for housing all the people who took advantage of his hospitality. While living in the ranch house as Wolf House was being built, he added a dining room with a fireplace. Twenty or more guests would routinely gather for the evening meal. For Wolf House, Jack planned a dining room that could seat fifty.

A few weeks before the Londons were to move into Wolf House, on the night of August 22, 1913, a great fire destroyed what had taken more than two years to build. Like the *Titanic*, Wolf House was thought to be indestructible, so no insurance had been taken on it. It was a terrible blow. The loss made Jack and Charmian depend upon each other, however. Four days after the fire, Charmian wrote in her diary: "Love is the order of the day, and in some ways we never were happier."

There was nothing for Jack to do but keep writing. Fortunately, this could be done while he took the medicine that seemed to help most during troubling times. In mid-October, Jack and Charmian boarded their thirty-foot yacht, the *Roamer*, for a two-and-a-half-month cruise along the mouths of the San Joaquin and Sacramento Rivers.

"Yours for the Revolution"

On April 16, 1914, Jack received a telegram. *Collier's* magazine was offering him eleven hundred dollars a week plus expenses to report on the Mexican Revolution, which had been brewing since 1910. The following day, he and Charmian left for Galveston, Texas. On April 24, Jack left Galveston for Vera Cruz, Mexico, only three days after troops from the United States took control of the port. The United States government feared that the civil war would spread northward.

This new assignment would help to pay the ranch bills. It would also be a test of Jack's commitment to socialism. The armies in rebellion against the Mexican dictator claimed that they were fighting against the capitalists' oppression of the working classes. Jack had long condemned oppression of workers around the world. However, he came to believe that in Mexico, the revolutionary leaders were only fighting for selfish personal gain.

Jack had long hoped to vindicate his ability as a war reporter following the disappointment of the Russo-Japanese War ten years earlier. He had no luck in Mexico, however, for there was virtually no fighting to report. The United States Army was content to safeguard the port of Vera Cruz and the important oil fields around Tampico. The only real fighting was guerrilla warfare deep in the interior of the country, and Jack never got near it.

The seven articles that Jack wrote showed how his opinion of the revolution changed. In the United States, socialists thought that their government was interfering in a true workers' revolt. Yet in Mexico, according to Jack, eighty

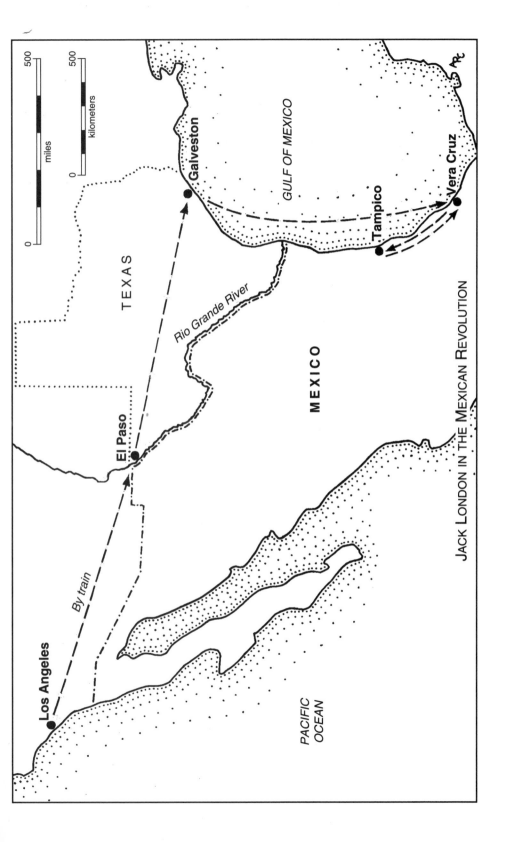

JACK LONDON IN THE MEXICAN REVOLUTION

percent of educated, middle-class Mexicans welcomed American intervention. They were tired of the problems created by the rebellion. The United States, he thought, was doing the right thing after all.

When Jack traveled to the oilfields of Tampico, he likened them to the rough-and-tumble Klondike during the gold days. He praised the order and skill of workers from the United States who were helping to develop Mexican resources. He also argued that Spain and Mexico had never developed any genius for government: "In a country where a man is legally considered guilty of a crime until he proves himself innocent, justice must mean an entirely different thing from what it means to an American."

Only five weeks after arriving in Mexico, Jack suffered a serious attack of dysentery which forced him to return to California. He had earned a lot of money but had not been successful in reporting the war. His major accomplishment had been to anger his socialist friends, who now saw him as speaking for racist American superiority.

The "Noseless One"

By 1914, Jack's fame was at its peak. He was the highest-paid writer in the United States. Even the works that some critics described as little more than extensive "notes for books" were very popular with readers. Motion pictures of his books and stories were showing in all parts of the country. Fame, however, could not bring Jack good health. By 1913, he sensed that the "noseless one"—his phrase for death—was never far away.

He had long suffered from stress and had recently been attacked by rheumatism, which caused his joints to ache and swell. He also knew that his kidneys were not working properly. (Some modern medical experts, after examining the record of Jack's health problems, have suggested that he

A well-dressed London poses for a portrait in 1909. (Trust of Irving Shepard)

actually suffered from the disease known as lupus, a disease not well known in his day. Lupus often affects the joints, skin, and kidneys.) By 1916 Jack became bloated, pale, and nervous. He no longer seemed his boyish self. His health problems were aggravated by his diet, for he loved to eat raw bonita fish and ducks which were barely cooked and hard to digest. Worst of all, Jack smoked heavily.

Beginning in February, 1915, Jack spent three-quarters of the rest of his life in Hawaii, where he could write and—he hoped—recover his health. On the beach at Waikiki he followed his usual routine. In the morning he would write his thousand words, and in the afternoon swim, play, or visit with friends. Seeing how well the landowners and their plantation laborers got along in Hawaii, he finally renounced his belief that workers could bring about better conditions for themselves. In March, 1916, he resigned from the Socialist Party. A few months later, he explained that "Liberty, Freedom and Independence are royal things that cannot be presented to, nor thrust upon, races or classes."

Jack still took immense pride in the ranch. While there, he enjoyed showing off his agricultural improvements to the enormous numbers of guests who dropped in. He was increasingly troubled by sleeplessness and by stomach and kidney problems, however, and thought that he must return to Hawaii for his health. On the morning of November 22, 1916, a few days before he was to leave, a servant tried to awaken him. Failing, he called doctors, who briefly aroused Jack before he slipped into his last coma.

"I LIKE"

Jack London's final explanation for everything was "I LIKE." He wrote the phrase in capital letters and treated it as if it were a biblical saying. What he meant by it was that people simply do what they most want to do. Even though people know all about what they are *supposed* to do, the instant that they say "I LIKE" something, nothing will stand in their way of doing it. Jack himself had always lived the way he wanted, rather than the way others thought he should. In the end, this philosophy of life finally delivered him to the "noseless one" at the age of forty.

Chapter 8

The American Dreamer

The cause of Jack London's death was probably heart failure and stroke. Because of his numerous medical problems, he might have died from any one of a number of ailments. However he died, it is clear that his lifestyle contributed to his death if it did not actually cause it.

An Early Death

In many ways, it is not surprising that the "noseless one" came early for Jack. He had always written about life as it was, not as people wished it could be. For most people, life was hard. They had to work long hours, six or seven days a week, to earn barely enough to survive. No company or government would take care of them. There would seldom be enough money for doctors when their health broke down. The system would then toss them aside, for they could no longer produce for their ten cents an hour. Jack had lived this life.

He was lucky to be strong and healthy as a young man, but he did not take good care of himself. Until he was nineteen, he did not own a toothbrush. He drank heavily as a teenager, which began to destroy his kidneys. He smoked from a very early age. The habit of smoking cigarettes, which he continued throughout his life, may have done more than anything else to bring about his death.

Even when Jack had choices, he did not make them with any regard for his health. Traveling to the Klondike, he came down with scurvy. Reporting the Russo-Japanese War, he was frostbitten. Sailing the Pacific, he contracted a variety of tropical diseases. In Mexico he suffered an acute attack of

The last photograph London posed for; it was taken less than two weeks before his death.
(Trust of Irving Shepard)

dysentery. He continually spent more money than he had, which put him under constant pressure to write what he knew he could sell—and to write a lot of it. The stress undoubtedly made every other problem worse.

Jack's creed always had been to live as a "superb meteor," with every atom "in magnificent glow," rather than as "a sleepy and permanent planet." He never tried to make his life longer by refusing to do the things he wanted. By committing himself absolutely to this way of thinking, he paid the price of an early death. His life is a prime example of living for the present.

People must make their own decisions about how to live their lives. They must decide for themselves if and when desires should be traded for security, or values for comfort. London's life shows the importance of thinking about such questions. How each person answers them will determine the crucial choices he or she makes in life.

Jack London as a Writer

Jack London is best remembered as one of the earliest writers of naturalism in the United States. While many authors were depicting the well-mannered life of the middle and upper classes, Jack wrote of people who struggled with their environment or with the harsh reality of their low place in society. London spent months or years learning the facts of a situation before writing about it. Most of his writing shows that people fight against social, economic, and biological forces that are largely beyond their control. Because this idea was becoming popular in the United States and Europe around the turn of the century, Jack's stories were enormously well received.

He was not popular simply because of his views, however. His style of writing is always strong and clear. Although he never graduated from high school, Jack was naturally intelligent and worked hard to improve his writing by studying the styles of other authors. He once suggested to an aspiring young writer: "Get your good strong phrases, fresh and vivid; write intensively, not exhaustively or lengthily; don't narrate—paint! draw! build! CREATE!" This was Jack's way of writing, and he did it as well as any author of his day.

He was a master in crafting sentences and paragraphs packed with meaning and power. He was less skillful at putting the paragraphs and plots together to create longer works in which every part worked together. As a result, his short stories and short novels are his best work, and he is principally remembered for them today.

The settings of Jack's stories and books also remain appealing to readers. At a time when most readers had few opportunities to leave their communities, they loved to read adventure stories about people who lived and traveled in exotic places. Because Jack had lived his life in such places, he could convince others that the characters he created were real people. Today, in an age when television, videos, and *National Geographic* photography can bring scenes of exciting distant places into the home, he is perhaps more admired for bringing a past age to life.

Jack's largest and most successful collection of writings came from his experience as a prospector in the Klondike region of Canada during 1897. Best-selling novels such as *The Call of the Wild* and *White Fang*, as well as dozens of stories, established him in the public mind as the "Kipling of the North." As early as 1901 he hoped to move on to other subjects, but the Klondike stories were still selling well. Jack will probably always be best known for his strong tales of the struggle for survival in the frozen Klondike.

The sea also brought out Jack's better qualities as an author. Because he developed a love of sailing early in life, he understood both the work it demanded and the magic it

Jack at the wheel of his thirty-foot boat the Roamer, *on which he and Charmian spent many happy months.* (Trust of Irving Shepard)

produced. The sea represented freedom, especially to a young boy tied to a depressing life in Oakland. Many other young boys and girls around the United States dreamed of escaping their own harsh circumstances as they read *The Cruise of the Dazzler* and *Tales of the Fish Patrol*.

The sea represented danger. No one who lived in Kansas or Kentucky all their lives had experienced a typhoon or harpooned a seal, but they could feel these experiences through Jack's writing. *The Sea-Wolf* and numerous newspaper and magazine articles made it clear that he understood the obstacles and possibilities the sea presented. Today, at a time when technology has eliminated so much danger from our lives, readers marvel at the courage of his characters.

The sea was also a highway to the unusual and exotic customs of people who lived in faraway places. By reading *The Cruise of the Snark, South Sea Tales*, and *On the Makaloa Mat*, ordinary people living regular lives could enjoy the experience of a stone-fishing expedition or thrill at the shout of "land, ho!" after two months at sea. Many times the public missed points that Jack wanted to make about society and the way people were treated, but they always sensed the reality of the scenes Jack painted of life in distant places.

Jack is also remembered for his pioneering work in the socialist movement in the United States. From the mid-1890's until his resignation from the Socialist Party in 1916, he threw his heart into the cause of the worker. Jack had experienced the life of the work-beast and felt that no one should have to endure such conditions. He wrote many essays and articles on behalf of the socialist cause, often without pay.

Less well known are Jack's tales of fantasy fiction. Readers familiar with the modern work of Isaac Asimov, Arthur C. Clarke, and other writers of science fiction may be surprised to find some familiar themes. In *The Scarlet Plague*, Jack described the deadly effects of mutation in bacterial life; the book depicts a world driven back to the Stone Age. Some people believe that his novels *Before Adam* and *The Star Rover* should be considered science fiction classics.

Jack London, Representative American

Just as important as Jack London's legacy as a writer is the example he set for all people struggling with life's large questions. He was, like most people, full of contradictions. He claimed to be a realist who believed in a world that operated like a machine, according to scientific principles. Yet toward the end of his life he began to believe in a spiritual life. Marriage, he wrote before he met Charmian Kittredge, should be founded upon mutual aid and common purposes, not upon sickly, sentimental love. Yet his greatest happiness in life came when he fell into that altogether mysterious kind of love that he wished to deny.

In literature, Jack is best known for his naturalistic themes, in which people are often overwhelmed by huge forces that they can neither understand nor control. Yet he lived as a bold individualist who would not conform to the larger forces around him. He thought that a writer should stick to what was real in order to hold a mirror to the world. However, he frequently wrote of individuals who escaped their circumstances, sometimes in strange parts of the world, and sometimes in worlds of the future.

Jack was at one time deeply committed to the cause of socialism, yet he could never quite escape his belief in the capacity of individuals to raise themselves by their own efforts. While he was signing his letters "yours for the revolution" and shouting down capitalism from a stage, he was constantly attended by servants. He explained this by saying that, until the revolution came, there must be workers, and he could at least treat his with dignity.

Jack London was honest and generous. He did not look

down on people because they were strange or had bad reputations. He had a "genius for friendship" which was based upon a genuine interest in others. He once wrote that the "simple" remedy for many of the world's problems was service:

> Not one ignoble thought or act is demanded of any, of all men and women in the world, to make fair the world. The call is for nobility of thinking, nobility of doing. The call is for service, and such is the wholesomeness of it. He who serves all best serves himself.

This was perhaps the most unrealistic hope that London ever put on paper. Yet most people would agree that loving others,

---

London at His Best

The closing lines of The Call of the Wild *beautifully capture the essence of Jack London's style:*

And here may well end the story of Buck. . . . In the summers there is one visitor, however, to that valley, of which the Yeehats do not know. It is a great, gloriously coated wolf, like, and yet unlike, all other wolves. He crosses alone from the smiling timber land and comes down into an open space among the trees. Here a yellow stream flows from rotted moosehide sacks and sinks into the ground, with long grasses growing through it and vegetable mould overrunning it and hiding its yellow from the sun; and here he muses for a time, howling once, long and mournfully, ere he departs.

But he is not always alone. When the long winter nights come on and the wolves follow their meat into the lower valleys, he may be seen running at the head of the pack through the pale moonlight or glimmering borealis, leaping gigantic above his fellows, his great throat a-bellow as he sings a song of the younger world, which is the song of the pack.

---

and loving life itself, is a good start toward improving the human condition. In both of these, Jack London set a good example for the world.

Major Books

The Call of the Wild. New York: Macmillan, 1903. On one level, perhaps the greatest dog story ever written, narrating Buck's progressive transformation from a pampered pup in California to the leader of a primal pack of wolves in the harsh Yukon. On another level, London's masterpiece is about the hidden desire in all people to return to a simpler, less civilized life which may be less secure, but is also closer to the essence of life.

The Cruise of the Snark. New York: Macmillan, 1911. London's account of his exotic South Seas adventures during the famous voyage of 1907-1909.

The Iron Heel. New York: Macmillan, 1907. This futuristic novel is written as if a historian seven centuries in the future had discovered a fragment of a manuscript written by Ernest Everhard, leader of a revolt against a fascist government in the United States between 1912 and 1932. Many critics have seen in it the foreshadowing of the regimes of Adolf Hitler and Benito Mussolini.

The Jacket. London: Mills and Boon, 1915. Republished as *The Star Rover.* New York: Macmillan, 1915. This novel, based upon the experience of two convicts confined to the horrors of the straitjacket, was meant to expose the brutality of the prison system. London adds a series of astral projections in which the captive Darrell Standing relives parts of former lives. His past lives include the "herculean Dane" Ragnar Lodbrog, who becomes a Roman legionnaire present at the crucifixion of Christ; and Daniel Foss, a nineteenth-century castaway who lives on a desert island for eight years.

John Barleycorn. New York: Century, 1913. A novel of the subtle attractions and dangers of drinking alcoholic beverages. Basing it at least partly on his own experiences, London wrote it to promote prohibition, and it has regularly been recommended by Alcoholics Anonymous ever since.

The People of the Abyss. New York: Macmillan, 1903. London's account of his six-week stay in the poorest section of London, England, disguised as a broke and stranded American sailor. After living with the street people of England's greatest city, he argued that most were there, not because of laziness, but because of disease, accidents, or old age.

The Son of the Wolf: Tales of the Far North. New York: Houghton Mifflin, 1900. London's first book, a collection of short stories, vividly describes the adventures and harsh realities of grappling with the frozen Yukon. These stories are dominated by the Malemute Kid, the ideal frontiersman of the northland.

White Fang. New York: Macmillan, 1906. A companion novel to *The Call of the Wild*, telling the story of a brutal wolf-dog gradually being transformed into a civilized, humanized dog.

Time Line

1876   Jack London is born on January 12 in San Francisco.

1886   London meets Ina Coolbrith, head librarian at the Oakland
            Library, who introduces him to the world of books.

1889   At age thirteen, London has to go to work full time at a
            cannery.

1891   London buys the boat *Razzle Dazzle* and begins raiding
            oyster beds in Oakland Bay; later that year, he joins the Fish
            Patrol.

1892   London sails to Siberia on the *Sophia Sutherland* for the
            annual seal hunt.

1893   "Typhoon," London's first story to be published, appears in
            the *San Francisco Morning Call* after winning the
            newspaper's writing contest.

1894   London joins Jacob Coxey's march on Washington, D.C.; he
            spends thirty days in the Erie County Penitentiary.

1896   London becomes known as the "boy socialist" of Oakland;
            in the fall, enters the University of California in Berkeley;
            meets Mabel Applegarth, his first love.

1897-1898   London goes to the Klondike to prospect for gold; in
            October, 1897, his father dies; in May, 1898, scurvy forces
            London to return home.

1899   London receives 266 rejection slips from magazines; in
            October, the *Atlantic Monthly* pays $120 for his story "An
            Odyssey of the North."

1900   London marries Bessie Mae Maddern; publishes first
            collection of short stories, *The Son of the Wolf: Tales of the
            Frozen North.*

1902   In disguise, London lives among the poor in the East End of
            London, England; the experience produces the book *The
            People of the Abyss.*

1902-1903   London becomes established as one of the most popular
            writers in the United States, publishing six books as well as
            many stories.

1903	*The Call of the Wild* is published and becomes sensationally successful.
1904	London covers the Russo-Japanese War for the San Francisco *Examiner*; London is divorced from Bessie.
1905	London buys the first tract of his ranch in Glen Ellen, California; on November 18, he marries Charmian Kittredge.
1907-1909	London, with Charmian, sails the South Seas for twenty-seven months aboard the *Snark*.
1909	London publishes the autobiographical novel *Martin Eden*.
1910	Joy London, Jack and Charmian's baby daughter, dies only two days after her birth.
1912	London sails from Baltimore to Seattle via Cape Horn on the barque *Dirigo*.
1913	Wolf House, after being under construction for two years, is destroyed by fire.
1914	London covers the Mexican Revolution for *Collier's* magazine; his fame is at its peak.
1915	Living in Hawaii, London tries to regain his health.
1916	On November 22, London dies at his ranch.

Glossary

Astrology: The belief that people's lives are influenced by the positions and movements of the moon and planets.

Capitalism: An economic system in which the production and distribution of goods is privately controlled for profit.

Common-law marriage: A marriage in which two people have not been legally married but live together and consider themselves married.

Estuary: An inlet or arm of the sea, especially at the wide mouth of a river.

Finishing school: A private girls' school that teaches manners, etiquette, and social skills to help prepare girls for life in upper-class society.

Freethinker: A person who forms opinions through his or her own reasoning and acts independently of the accepted views of society.

Ice wagon: Before the days of refrigeration, a wagon that brought large chunks of ice to people's houses for preserving food.

Individualism: The belief that people should be guided by self-interest according to their own values and that the interests of the individual are of prime importance.

Industrialization: The use of machine power to produce goods more efficiently, often involving large factories with many workers; it became widespread in the United States beginning in the 1860's.

Klondike: A gold-mining region along the Klondike River in what is today the Yukon Province of Canada; about the size of the state of Ohio.

Leprosy: An infectious tropical disease that causes skin lesions, numbness, paralysis, deformities, and the destruction of muscle tissue; in London's time, there was no cure.

Mackintosh: A type of raincoat made of fabric and rubber fused together.

Naturalism: A type of writing popular around 1900 that portrayed life according to modern scientific truth as it was understood at the time; emphasized the power of great economic, social, and biological forces and the powerlessness of individuals.

Psoriasis: A skin disease that causes red patches and white, scaly skin.

Racism: The belief that character, intelligence, and other similar traits are based upon one's race, usually with the suggestion that one race is superior to another; there is no scientific basis for this belief.

Rough: A rowdy or coarse person without refined manners.

Russo-Japanese War: A war between Russia and Japan in 1904 and 1905 over economic interests in Korea and northern China (Manchuria);

established Japan as a world power.

Schooner: A type of sailing ship with two masts (the poles that hold the sails), a foremast and a mainmast.

Scurvy: A disease that causes bleeding into the skin and membranes and that weakens the gums; caused by a lack of vitamin C.

Sloop: A type of sailing ship with one mast.

Socialism: An economic system in which the production and distribution of goods is controlled by the government so that, ideally, all members of society are cared for adequately.

Spiritualism: The belief that the dead survive as spirits that can communicate with the living.

The *Titanic*: A luxurious ocean liner, launched in 1912, that was considered "unsinkable"; it sank on its maiden voyage after hitting an iceberg.

Vagrant: A person who wanders from place to place without a regular job.

Yacht: A relatively small sailing ship with graceful lines and a sharp prow (front), usually used for recreation.

Bibliography

Kingman, Russ. *A Pictorial Life of Jack London.* New York: Crown, 1979. This biography of London is accessible to a young adult audience. Kingman takes a strictly chronological approach and deals directly with many of the controversial questions about London's life. Especially valuable for its more than 250 pictures and illustrations. Written by the executive director of the Jack London Foundation.

Labor, Earle. *Jack London.* New York: Twayne, 1974. The best study of all Jack London's books. Written by a leading London scholar.

Labor, Earle, Robert C. Leitz III, and I. Milo Shepard, eds. *The Letters of Jack London.* 3 vols. Stanford, Calif.: Stanford University Press, 1988. Contains more than 1,500 letters written by London throughout his life. Particularly important because it includes many early letters for the first time and because it corrects misleading impressions left by editors of London letters published earlier. Objective and fully annotated.

Lane, Frederick A. *The Greatest Adventure: A Story of Jack London.* New York: Aladdin Books, 1954. This is an overly simplistic study of Jack as a boy with an adventuresome spirit. It is misleading in many places and never truly deals with London's troubled childhood. It is widely available, however, and is typical of many earlier studies for young people.

London, Charmian K. *The Book of Jack London.* 2 vols. New York: Century, 1921. Written by London's wife, this is a necessary study because of the unique perspective she provides. It is, however, highly favorable to London and conceals many things.

London, Joan. *Jack London and His Times: An Unconventional Biography.* New York: Doubleday, Doran, 1939. This biographical study was written by London's eldest daughter, with whom he attempted to develop cordial relations but did not succeed. It is a good account of his political activity but is somewhat biased about his personal life.

Schroeder, Alan. *Jack London.* New York: Chelsea House, 1991. A biography written specifically for young adults. It is accurate and corrects many false impressions of earlier biographies written for this group.

Sinclair, Andrew. *Jack: A Biography of Jack London.* New York: Harper & Row, 1977. Sinclair focuses on London's medical problems and suggests that his adventurous spirit and writing declined as a result.

Stone, Irving. *Sailor on Horseback: The Biography of Jack London.*
Boston: Houghton Mifflin, 1938. This is probably the most widely
circulated biography of London. It is full of atmosphere, but not reliable,
containing more than two hundred errors. Emphasizes London's concern
about his illegitimate birth.

Walker, Franklin. *Jack London and the Klondike: The Genesis of an
American Writer.* San Marino, Calif.: The Huntington Library, 1966.
Deals with London's Klondike experiences as the turning point in his
life. Demonstrates that the best of London's writing was drawn from his
own experience.

Media Resources

Anderson, Bob, producer. *Jack London's California*. Film. San Francisco: KGO, 1984. In this dramatization, filmed for San Francisco's Public Broadcasting Service station, Martin Sheen plays the mature Jack London, and Charlie Sheen portrays him as a young man.

The Call of the Wild. Film, 1976. Novelist and poet James Dickey wrote the script for this adaptation, filmed as a movie for television. John Beck and Bernard Fresson star in this stark and effective version of the story.

Jack London's "To Build a Fire." Film or video, 15 minutes. 1975. Distributed by Bureau of Audio Visual Instruction, University of Wisconsin, Madison. A re-creation of London's famous story of an inexperienced newcomer to the Yukon who is progressively destroyed by his lack of survival skills.

Powell, Marykay, producer. *White Fang*. Video, 109 minutes. Walt Disney Pictures, 1991. Distributed by Buena Vista. A retelling of London's story of a boy who returns to the Yukon Territory to fulfill his father's wish. It is a moving story of the friendship between a wolf-dog and a boy learning to be a man. Beautifully filmed on location by director Randal Kleiser.

Warner, Jack, and Hal B. Wallis, producers. *The Sea Wolf*. Film, 100 minutes. 1941. Directed by Michael Curtiz, this is a classic Hollywood version of the London novel. Edward G. Robinson gives a fine sneering performance as Wolf Larsen. The film emphasizes action over the philosophizing that pervades the novel.

Zanuck, Darryl F., producer. *Call of the Wild*. Film, 89 minutes. 1935. Available on video, this version of the London novel has been called "more Hollywood than Jack London," but it is good, old-style film entertainment. Directed by William Wellman, it stars Clark Gable and Loretta Young.

The Arts

JACK LONDON

INDEX